Silence

Praise for Storyshares

"One of the brightest innovators and game-changers in the education industry."
– Forbes

"Your success in applying research-validated practices to promote literacy serves as a valuable model for other organizations seeking to create evidence-based literacy programs."
- Library of Congress

"We need powerful social and educational innovation, and Storyshares is breaking new ground. The organization addresses critical problems facing our students and teachers. I am excited about the strategies it brings to the collective work of making sure every student has an equal chance in life."
– Teach For America

"It's the perfect idea. There's really nothing like this. I mean, wow, this will be a wonderful experience for young people."
- Andrea Davis Pinkney, Executive Director, Scholastic

"Reading for meaning opens opportunities for a lifetime of learning. Providing emerging readers with engaging texts that are designed to offer both challenges and support for each individual will improve their lives for years to come. Storyshares is a wonderful start."
- David Rose, Co-founder of CAST & UDL

Silence

Lisa Zhang

A Storyshares book

Storyshares

Story Share, Inc.

24 N. Bryn Mawr Avenue #340

Bryn Mawr, PA 19010-3304

www.storyshares.org

Inspiring reading with a new kind of book.

Interest Level: High School

Grade Level Equivalent: 3

9798885978095

Book design by Storyshares

Storyshares Presents

Chapter One

I DROVE THE CAR into the parking lot. I twisted halfway in my seat to look at my child. Really *look* at her, in a way only a mother could.

She sat with her hair tied back into a tight, high ponytail. Her posture was stiff. Her toes pointed upward like they were straining to reach the sky. Her hands were locked around her backpack straps.

She looked as well as any kid could who was about to enter sixth grade at a new school that spoke a foreign language. The nervousness her body showed did not reflect on her calm face.

A surge of pride went through my body. I smiled.

"Good luck!" I said in English. I threw every ounce of excitement into those two words.

I studied English literature at Guangdong's state university in China. That was back in the late eighties. It was a time when I was too busy making sure I filled my stomach every night to care about my educational progress.

If I had known that our survival would now depend on it, I might've tried harder.

Adeline tried to smile, and wordlessly got out of the car.

We'd only been in our new apartment for three days, but I'd already made myself look like a fool more than I'd done my whole life. This morning, a few strangers watched with their lips curled as I made the cashier repeat *five* times how much the change was. Finally, she grabbed a piece of paper from under the desk, wrote two large numbers with a red marker, and dangled it in front of my face. I quickly paid and escaped from the store.

I felt my face heat again. I made my quick retreat from that part of my mind. Pressing a palm to my forehead, I shut my eyes.

I need a break, I thought. *The Bahamas sounds like a mighty good idea...*

Then I drifted into a peaceful nothingness.

Chapter Two

"　　　? H<small>OW WAS THE</small> first day?" I asked in both Chinese and English.

Adeline mumbled something under her breath.

"　　What?" I asked again.

Am I losing my mind? I wondered. *First the cashier, now Adeline.*

"Fine," she said, louder this time.

"Okay," I said, copying her one-word answer.

I was too relieved that she spoke in English to think about the vague answer.

Sitting up from a slump, I started the car and drove us home. Though there were a thousand questions in my mind, we stayed silent.

When I could take it no longer, I took a deep breath. I looked at the reflection of Adeline in the rearview mirror.

"Adeline," I started.

My eyes narrowed. They focused on a rectangular, sharp-edged object held against her chest.

"　　What is that?" I asked.

"A book," she said, tightening her arms.

I blinked.

It's the first day of school, and already she wants to read an English book? I wondered.

In college, our readings were all children's books — *The Cat in the Hat* was my favorite.

I shook my head.

This is too good to be real, I thought.

I focused on Adeline in the rearview mirror again. She was peeking at me from under lowered lashes. She was most likely waiting for my reaction.

My lips parted, and a wide grin broke across my face.

Her hunched shoulders relaxed. She really had nothing to fear. Quite the opposite.

Never mind about the Bahamas. I knew, deep down, that even the softest sand and the bluest ocean couldn't get rid of my fear that my sweet Adeline would refuse to give our new life a chance. Just the sight of her with an English book made my head swim with relief. I could hardly stay in my lane as I finally pulled into the garage. Unbuckling the seatbelt and twisting around, I said, "Adeline—"

She was already out the door and running for the house.

My eyes dimmed a bit.

It's fine, I decided. *She brought a book with her. An English one.*

That was all I needed to sleep soundly that night.

Chapter Three

THE NEXT WEEK WAS the same. Adeline would go to school, clutch a new book to her chest in the car, and run up to her room as soon as I unlocked the car door. The only time she left her room was to eat at 6:00.

I stayed silent, of course. I didn't want to risk breaking whatever magic she found in those books.

My attempts at conversation failed anyway. Any questions I asked in Chinese were ignored. Any I tried in English got almost the same response. It's hard to keep a conversation going when all you get are one-word grunts.

It was yet another Friday when I banged on Adeline's bedroom door. I was gathering every last bit of motherly authority to tell her to join me for dinner.

Silence answered me.

Stomping and huffing in frustration, I went back to the dining table. I started eating the food. Let her get lost in her damned books.

Another half an hour passed before I finally heard the opening click of a door. I looked around as Adeline came down the stairs. With unusual grace, she walked to her seat across from mine.

I studied her. Her eyes were wide and unfocused. She looked like her mind and body were in two different places. I guessed that her mind was still in all the pages she was flipping through.

She looked down at the food. She blinked, then frowned.

I was getting a little unnerved.

"What?" I asked.

She blinked again. Confusion flashed in her eyes for a split second. Then they cleared completely.

"Nothing," she said quietly, and picked up the chopsticks.

Conversation over.

I kept staring at her. I felt like I was peeling away an invisible mask that had been carefully weaved. It was strange for her to keep this silence. I hadn't let it bother me for the past few days, but now...

Why is she acting like this? My mind started to race. *Is she closing in on herself? Has she given up?*

Each question was more unsettling than the last. I scrambled to get rid of the uncomfortable feeling in the room.

"How was school?" I asked in both English and Chinese.

I remembered how well she had once responded to Chinese only.

Her chopsticks stopped in midair as her chewing slowed.

I held my breath.

After a few, painful seconds, she said, "It was raining cats and dogs the whole day, so we didn't play outside. But math class was..."

She finished the sentence with a word I didn't understand.

In fact, the whole sentence made little sense. My brain worked hard to translate each word, but I quickly stopped.

"It was raining cats and dogs?" I echoed.

There's no way those books are taking away her ability to speak correctly, is there? I wondered.

"Oh, yes," she said. She nodded like she was making a point.

My expression must have turned worried.

Adeline snapped, "What?"

I had the feeling that I was on dangerous ground. I thought about letting it go. Right now did not seem like a good time to fight with each other. But my mouth betrayed me.

"Can you talk normally?" I asked in Chinese.

I had put down my chopsticks and snapped right back. My eyes shot invisible daggers across the table.

She just stared blankly back and tilted her head.

That move made my blood boil with anger.

She will not pretend she doesn't understand, to make me speak English, I thought. *Not this time.*

So I stared right back, using the same weapon: silence. Two can play the game.

Except Adeline refused to break.

I snorted. At least she kept that spark of defiance, no matter how many books she read. A wave of sudden relief washed over me. It was so strong that I gave in.

I asked again in English, "Can you talk normally?"

"I am," she answered.

I was on edge all over again.

Now, it was her turn to look at me with worry.

Before I could say anything else, she set her chopsticks down. She pushed back her chair. She walked past me and went upstairs to her bedroom, where another world was waiting for her.

I stared down at my plate, at the half-eaten pop-tart.

I lost all my appetite.

Chapter Four

WE DIDN'T SPEAK FOR the rest of the week.

While Adeline was too lost in her books to care, I was angry. My glares were answered with a carelessness that only made me more angry.

I couldn't remember why I had ever been relieved to see Adeline clutching a book to her chest like a lifeline. Now I blamed them for the widening gap between us.

I was still lost in thought as I drove back from dropping her off at school. I remembered it was Monday. Time to clear out the trash.

Heaving a huge sigh, I walked upstairs toward Adeline's bedroom. I was already dreading what I would find.

Books of all shapes and sizes were littered over the floor and on every surface. My throat tightened.

This has gone too far, a voice inside my head said.

But isn't this what you wanted? another voice asked.

I shook my head. I didn't look any further. I went to the trash can in the far corner. It was half-hidden under the bed.

I reached for the trash can, but something caught my eye. Among a sea of crumpled white paper, a sliver of pink stood out. It was the size of a tennis ball, like someone had crushed it with all their strength.

I carefully pulled it out, cringing as I stuck my hand into the trash. Unfolding the paper, I smoothed over the crinkled edges.

I could read "Parent Night, September 30th, 6-8 pm" printed in big, black letters across the top.

I inhaled sharply. That was two weeks ago.

Why didn't Adeline tell me? I wondered. This would've been a great chance to bond with our neighbors.

My hands curled into fists. When Adeline came back, she would have some things to answer for.

Chapter Five

A TAP ON THE window. I unlocked the car door.

Adeline slid into the backseat, silent as always.

I was the same today. If I opened my mouth, I probably would've started shouting.

I drove into the garage and turned off the car. I just waited.

Adeline pulled the door handle to escape to her room, but I stopped her.

"Wait," I said in Chinese. "I need to talk to you."

Maybe it was my too-calm voice or my murderous expression, but Adeline obeyed. She followed me into the living room as we entered the house together.

I motioned for her to sit down. She sat.

Without saying anything, I took the pink paper from my jacket pocket. I laid it on the table.

Her eyes widened.

That proved it. She had known, and had not told me.

"Why didn't you tell me?" I asked, still in Chinese.

Adeline bit her lip. "I forgot," she mumbled.

I snorted. The most pathetic excuse the world has ever known. She wanted to avoid the subject, but my patience was used up.

I said in English, her preferred language, "If you don't tell me the truth, I will take all your books."

The moment those words left my tongue, I knew I'd upset her.

She fidgeted. Her nostrils flared.

Good. Desperation is one way to make people be honest. It wasn't the most merciful way, but I was past that.

She snapped, "You wouldn't have been helpful anyway, so what's the point?"

I blinked. That was unexpected.

"What do you mean?" I asked.

Adeline took a deep breath and went on. "I doubt you would have understood anything they said, so I didn't feel the need to tell you about it," she said.

That got another blink from me. The words rang in my ear but didn't sink in. She spoke way too fast.

"What?" I asked in Chinese.

Adeline looked like I had just proved her point.

She spoke again, dragging each word out and pausing between words. "I... doubt... you... would... have... understood... what... was... going... on," she said.

I didn't react to the rudeness of her tone, especially as the meaning of her words finally sank in. I blinked again, but it wasn't from confusion this time. So many thoughts swarmed in my head at once that I found it hard to breathe.

When I pulled myself together and came back to my senses, Adeline had already left.

I knew my English skills were nowhere near fluent. Adeline had spoken the truth. Though having it said out loud hurt a little, that wasn't what shocked me. It was the idea behind what she said.

I am to blame. I should know everything. I am not doing enough.

No, I thought. I shook my head. *This is not right at all.*

I needed a plan, and fast.

An hour later, I came out of the bookstore. I was holding a new copy of a *Collins-Robert French Dictionary*.

Chapter Six

I WAITED.

My plan depended on Adeline speaking to me first. It took all my self-control not to say a word to her for another three days.

She truly wants nothing to do with me, I thought.

It was a bitter thought that I pushed away quickly.

At last, my silence was rewarded on a hot Friday afternoon. I was relaxing on the sofa, scrolling on my phone, when Adeline came downstairs.

It was a very rare sight, but I didn't react to her being there. That is, until her footsteps got closer.

I still didn't react. But I thought to myself, *This is it. Play it right.*

"Can I go to Clare's house tomorrow?" she finally asked. "It's the weekend."

Saying each word clearly, I answered, *"non, vous ne peux pas."*

(No, you can't.)

She blinked. I could almost see her little brain working to figure it out. "What?" she asked.

I repeated, *"Non, vous ne peux pas."*

"What are you saying?" Adeline asked, frowning.

She looked disturbed. Good.

"Tu dois arrêter" was my answer. *(You have to stop.)*

She took a step back. She looked worried now.

"Are you mad?" she asked. Her voice was shaking, just a little. "Can you talk normally?"

I almost lost control, then. Talk normally? *Talk normally?* She'd been the one refusing to speak her native language for the past month.

I felt my blood heat. I almost forgot the few phrases I'd managed to memorize. My progress was slow and pathetic, but I'd learned enough to prove my point.

I repeated the word that best showed my anger: *"Non." (No.)*

Adeline had the nerve to look just as pissed.

"I don't know what you are doing," she said, "but you need to stop it."

I refused.

"Un, deux, trois, quatre, cinq, six, sept…" I started to chant the numbers. My voice was rising in the air.

"Stop!" Adeline screamed. *"Stop! What is wrong with you?"*

Chinese. Finally.

I snorted, a sound mixed with anger and relief. "You can still speak Chinese?" I asked.

Adeline asked after a moment of quiet, "What do you want?"

"Speak Chinese," I said.

A simple request.

Speak Chinese.

It was something that should not be hard to accept if she respected her mother and her heritage.

She thought for another moment. Then she answered, "I'll try."

I was caught off guard. The agreement was so quick, I didn't care that she spoke in English again. I had come prepared for battle, not a peaceful truce with no bloodshed.

I asked if she was serious, even if that made me sound like an idiot.

"Yes," Adeline said, sighing.

It was a long, heavy exhale through her nose that had me blinking in surprise again. It made her seem ten years older, that move.

"I think I know what you are trying to say," she explained. "It's hard. I've always wanted to fit in, now more than ever. I thought you would get in the way of that. So I stayed away. But I suppose it's not fair to you, since you are not to blame for anything. So I'll try to be better." She shrugged, going for casual.

It was more words than Adeline had given me all week, though I understood only half of it.

She is truly becoming a natural, I thought to myself.

When I expected a moment of worry to hit me, there was none.

That was when I realized there was nothing I needed to worry about.

Yes, Adeline and I were growing apart. Yes, we were more quiet around each other now. But we could still have a good mother-daughter relationship.

That bond will never be broken, even though it might change.

So I looked at my daughter again. I let more warmth into my eyes than I'd given her for the past week.

I said, "We will both try."

About the Author

Lisa Zhang is an ardent writer who moved from China to Irvine, California in sixth grade. She loves reading, playing volleyball and exercising in her neighborhood. She hopes to spread love and joy through writing fiction, non-fiction and opinion pieces.

About the Publisher

Story Shares is a nonprofit focused on supporting the millions of teens and adults who struggle with reading by creating a new shelf in the library specifically for them. The ever-growing collection features content that is compelling and culturally relevant for teens and adults, yet still readable at a range of lower reading levels.

Story Shares generates content by engaging deeply with writers, bringing together a community to create this new kind of book. With more intriguing and approachable stories to choose from, the teens and adults who have fallen behind are improving their skills and beginning to discover the joy of reading. For more information, visit storyshares.org.

Easy to Read. Hard to Put Down.